P9-DNB-499

The Boy Who Saved Cleveland

THE BOY
WHO SAVED
CLEVELAND

Based on a True Story

JAMES CROSS GIBLIN

illustrated by
MICHAEL DOOLING

HENRY HOLT AND COMPANY
NEW YORK

Henry Holt and Company, LLC
Publishers since 1866
175 Fifth Avenue
New York, New York 10010
www.henryholtchildrensbooks.com

Henry Holt® is a registered trademark of Henry Holt and Company, LLC.
Text copyright © 2006 by James Cross Giblin
Illustrations copyright © 2006 by Michael Dooling
All rights reserved.
Distributed in Canada by H. B. Fenn and Company Ltd.

Library of Congress Cataloging-in-Publication Data
Giblin, James Cross.
The boy who saved Cleveland : based on a true story / by James Cross Giblin;
illustrated by Michael Dooling.—1st ed.
p.   cm.
Summary: During a malaria epidemic in late eighteenth-century Cleveland, Ohio,
ten-year-old Seth Doan surprises his family, his neighbors, and himself by having the
strength to carry and grind enough corn to feed everyone. Based on a true story.
ISBN-13: 978-0-8050-7355-3 / ISBN-10: 0-8050-7355-8
1. Ohio—History—18th century—Juvenile fiction.
[1. Ohio—History—18th century—Fiction. 2. Frontier and pioneer life—Ohio—
Fiction. 3. Self-confidence—Fiction. 4. Epidemics—Fiction. 5. Sick—Fiction.
6. Malaria—Fiction.] I. Dooling, Michael, ill. II. Title.
PZ7.G33925345Boy 2006   [Fic]—dc22   2005021695

First Edition—2006
The artist used pencil on paper to create the illustrations for this book.
Printed in the United States of America on acid-free paper. ∞

1 3 5 7 9 10 8 6 4 2

For the city of Cleveland,
which gave me so much as I was growing up
—J. C. G.

>—·◆>—·○—·◆·—·—<

To Kevin, Jr.
—M. D.

ACKNOWLEDGMENTS

*Thanks are due the library staff and facilities
of the Western Reserve Historical Society in Cleveland, Ohio,
where I did much of the research for this story. A book that was
especially helpful was* The Cuyahoga, a History of the
Northern Ohio River, *by William Donohue Ellis, New York:
Holt, Rinehart and Winston, 1966; reprinted 1985 by Landfall
Press, Inc., Dayton, Ohio. The book is available online.*

CONTENTS

INTRODUCTION

If you could look down on the place from the air, you might think no one lived there. Thick, unbroken forest stretches to the east, west, and south as far as the eye can see. To the north, a river empties into the blue-gray waters of Lake Erie.

But if you looked more closely, you'd spot a tiny settlement near the mouth of the river. Three log cabins stand in a clearing carved out of the forest. Surrounding them are a few acres planted with corn. From above, the corn plants look like a lush green carpet.

This is Cleveland, Ohio, as it was in the late summer of 1798, more than two hundred years ago. At a distance, it seems peaceful, even beautiful. But a terrible sickness is about to descend on the settlement—a sickness that could threaten its very existence. . . .

CHAPTER ONE

The Shakes and Fever

Flies buzzed in the hot room, but Seth Doan didn't notice them. The magical words he was reading carried him far away from the cabin on the Ohio frontier.

"And Abraham rose up early in the morning, and saddled his ass, and took two of his young men with him, and Isaac his son. . . ." Once again Seth was caught up in the story of Abraham and Isaac. It was one of his favorites in the family Bible—the only book the Doans had brought with them on their long journey from Connecticut to northern Ohio.

Seth didn't have much time for reading. Most days he was busy with chores from the time the sun rose until it set. If he wasn't hauling water from the spring for his mother, he was helping his father clear more land to plant corn. Or he was off fishing for perch and pike in the shallow waters of Lake Erie.

Today was different, though. After the noon meal, when the late July sun had risen high in the sky, his father had turned to Seth and said, "Why don't you stay inside and rest this afternoon, son?"

"But we need Seth's help in the cornfield," his mother protested. "We can't clear out the rest of the weeds by ourselves."

"Mercy can help us," his father said, quietly but firmly. Mercy was Seth's older sister.

His mother had frowned. "You spoil the boy," she said. "It won't hurt Seth to sweat a little." She ruffled her son's hair.

"I don't mind working outside," Mercy said. "Maybe there'll be a breeze." She had spent the morning cleaning the airless cabin.

And so it was settled. While Mercy joined her

parents in the cornfield, Seth sat on a stool near the cabin door to read the story of Abraham and Isaac. "And they came to a place which God had told him of; and Abraham built an altar there, and laid the wood in order, and bound Isaac his son, and laid him on the altar upon the wood."

Seth had read the story at least a hundred times. But he still felt a chill when he got to this part, about the sacrifice of Isaac. Just then he heard something from outside that sent a different kind of chill through him. It was his mother's voice. "Mercy!" she screamed.

Seth jumped up from the stool as his father hurried across the yard, carrying Mercy in his arms. His mother followed close behind. "What happened?" Seth asked fearfully as they pushed past him into the cabin.

"Mercy groaned," his mother said. "And then she fainted."

"What's wrong with her?"

"Don't know," Seth's father said. He laid Mercy gently on her pallet in a far corner. "She started

shivering," Seth's mother said. "Then she broke out in a terrible sweat."

"We're afraid it may be the shakes and fever," Seth's father said, his voice low and anxious. He pulled a blanket up over Mercy, who had already dozed off.

Seth shuddered. The shakes and fever was one of the worst ailments a person could get. It latched itself onto you and wouldn't let go.

His father rose to his feet. "I'd best get back to work," he said.

"I'll stay here and look after Mercy," Seth's mother said. "Seth can go out to the field with you."

Mr. Doan turned to Seth. "I'm sorry to take you away from your reading, son," he said. "But I do need your help."

"All right, Pa," Seth said. He couldn't help sighing, though, as he put the Bible away on its special shelf.

His mother heard him. "Why are you sighing?" she said. "You got what you wanted, sitting here in the cabin and reading while we all slaved in the hot sun."

"Eliza . . . ," Seth's father said gently.

But his mother wasn't to be stopped. "Maybe if you'd gone with us in the first place your sister wouldn't have gotten sick!"

"That's enough, Eliza," his father cut in. "Seth hasn't done anything wrong. You know he tires easily. I wanted him to have the afternoon off."

Seth backed away toward the fireplace. Why did his parents have to quarrel—and especially about him?

"You're too easy on Seth," his mother said.

"Maybe I am," Mr. Doan said, reaching out to embrace his wife. "But he's the only son I have left."

Mrs. Doan looked up at her husband's sad expression. "Don't you think he's my son, too?" She began to cry, and Mr. Doan hugged her tighter.

Seth couldn't stand it any longer. He slipped through the cabin door without his parents seeing him, and stood for a moment looking around the clearing. Then, not knowing what else to do, he headed for the cornfield. He couldn't understand why his mother was so angry. Back in Connecticut, she'd always been the one who encouraged him to read.

CHAPTER TWO

What's Happened to Pa?

Seth saw where his family had stopped weeding, and bent down to pull out the next unwanted plant. He yanked it up, making sure he got all the roots, shook off the dirt, and tossed the plant aside. Then he moved on to the next, and repeated his actions—yank, shake, toss.

Today he didn't mind the boring work. The hot sun burning through his shirt didn't bother him either. They helped him forget what had made his father sad and his mother cry. First the twins, Ethan and Matthew, had died of the lung fever while the family was still living in Connecticut.

And then baby Thomas had wasted away of the colic in June, just two months ago.

Thomas had been such a sweet baby, always smiling and cheerful. And now he was buried just beyond the cornfield, under a tall oak tree. If Seth had turned around, he could have seen the simple wooden cross on Thomas's grave. But he didn't look that way for fear it would make him cry, too. Instead he pulled up another weed.

"Why are you working in that row, son?" Seth shaded his eyes and saw his father striding toward the cornfield. "Let me weed it," Mr. Doan said. "You can do the last row, where you'll get a little shade from the woods."

Seth bristled. There his father went again, treating him as if he were weak—a baby like Thomas who always needed to be protected. Couldn't he see that he, Seth, was ten, and able to work as hard as anyone? But he didn't say anything. Why upset his father all over again?

Seth went to work in the last row, finished weeding it, and then moved on to the next one. Every once in a while he'd look up to see his

father, four rows over, bending down and rising up just as Seth was doing. To make the work more interesting, Seth pretended he was running a kind of race with his father. He speeded up his pace—yank, shake, toss—trying to move more quickly than Mr. Doan.

Seth stopped for a moment to catch his breath and looked across the rows. He saw nothing but cornstalks, standing tall in the windless air. "Pa?" he called. No answer. He called again: "Pa?" Still no answer.

Where had his father gone? Seth ran to the end of his row, across the top of the field near Thomas's grave, and down the row where his father had been weeding. Mr. Doan was struggling to rise to his feet.

"Pa!" Seth hurried to him.

"I don't know what came over me," Mr. Doan said shakily. "One moment I was bending down to pull out a weed, the next I was lying in the dirt."

Mr. Doan tried to take a step forward, but wobbled unsteadily. "The field is spinning round," he said.

Seth grabbed hold of his father's left arm. "Lean on me," he said. He led his father out of the field and over to a tree stump.

"The sun must have gotten to me." Mr. Doan smiled weakly. "Don't worry, son. I'll be all right in a minute."

In less time than that, his father rose to his feet. Beads of perspiration stood out on his forehead and his face was pale under its tan. But he moved forward with determination. "I just need to lie down for a while," he said.

Seth reached out to help him. "That's all right," his father said, brushing Seth aside. "I can make it on my own."

Seth let his father walk on ahead, but he felt uneasy. First Mercy had taken ill, and now Pa had come down with something. Seth surely hoped it would be cured by a little rest, whatever it was. But he couldn't shake off a sense of dread as he followed his father toward the cabin.

CHAPTER THREE

To the Mill

The cabin was quiet when Seth woke up the next morning. That was odd, he thought. Most mornings he could hear his father and mother talking downstairs. Or else his sister would be singing. Then he remembered. . . .

Seth rose from his straw mattress. Being careful not to bump his head on the attic's sloping roof, he pulled on his shirt and pants. Then he climbed down the ladder to the cabin's single room.

His mother was wringing out a cloth in a pail of water. "Where's Pa?" Seth asked.

"Sh-h-h-h," his mother said. "Your father's

come down with the shakes and fever, too. And Mercy's worse." She nodded toward the corner of the cabin where Seth's sister lay, wrapped in a blanket.

"Mornin', Seth," Mercy whispered.

Seth was shocked. Could this weak-sounding girl be his jolly sister? "I hope you're feeling better," he said, but he didn't know if Mercy heard him. She had closed her eyes again.

Mrs. Doan lifted a curtain at the other end of the room. Behind it Seth's father lay on the cabin's only bed, which was built into the wall. "I've got to get up!" the man said. Seth could see that he was shivering.

"That'll just make it worse," Seth's mother said. She bathed her husband's forehead with the damp cloth. "You must rest."

"But who'll go to the mill to grind our corn?" Mr. Doan asked. He turned on his side and tried to sit up. "We'll have nothing to eat if I don't!"

When the Doans arrived in Cleveland, their neighbor Lorenzo Carter had loaned them seed corn from last year's crop to plant in the field they cleared. Meanwhile, they were using some of the borrowed corn to help tide them over until their own crop was ready to harvest.

The Doans ate other things: squirrels and rabbits that Mr. Doan hunted, fish that he and Seth caught in the lake, wild fruits and berries that the family gathered from the woods. Corn was their mainstay, though—corn for mush, and corn for bread. But first the hard kernels had to be ground into meal.

"I'll go to the mill," Seth's mother said to her husband. "Now you just lie back down." Mr. Doan obeyed her reluctantly, and she pulled the blanket up over his chest.

Seth could see how tired his mother was. With both Pa and Mercy sick, how could she leave them to go to the mill? She had her hands full here at home.

Suddenly Seth heard himself saying, "I can go."

Mrs. Doan looked surprised, and then she smiled.

Seth's father raised up on an elbow. "No, son. That job is too hard for you. It takes a lot of

kernels to make a day's supply of meal. And they are heavier than you'd think. I'll get up and . . ."

Mr. Doan started to stand, but dropped back on the bed again. "I'm so dizzy all of a sudden," he said.

"Lie down!" Seth's mother commanded. "You're in no fit condition to go anywhere!" Then her tone softened and she patted her husband's shoulder. "Seth's stronger than you give him credit for," she said. "Maybe he can't carry as much corn as you, but he can carry enough to keep us fed."

Mr. Doan said nothing more as he got back under the covers. Mrs. Doan dropped the curtain beside his bed and turned to Seth. "Go now before your father wakes up again," she whispered. She gave him a quick hug. "You can do the job, Seth. I know you can."

"I'll try my best," he promised. But his hands shook as he filled a sack with kernels of corn from the storage bin behind the cabin. Why had he offered to go to Judge Kingsbury's mill? It was more than two miles from the settlement, and uphill all the way.

Wild animals lived in the thick woods that bordered the path. What would he do if he ran into a buck deer or an angry bear?

Stop imagining things, he told himself. He'd made a promise to his mother, and he intended to keep it. With a sigh, he hoisted the heavy sack of corn onto his back and started out.

CHAPTER FOUR

Sickness Everywhere

Next door, a thin trail of smoke rose from the Stiles family's chimney as Seth passed their cabin. It was too early for the Stileses' little girls to be out playing in the yard.

Seth was careful to avoid Mrs. Stiles's flower bed. He'd never seen anyone explode in anger the way she had when he ran across it one day and accidentally flattened a few petunias. The last thing he wanted now was another tongue-lashing from his neighbor.

All was quiet around Lorenzo Carter's cabin, too. The Carter place was the largest of the three cabins in Cleveland. It had two rooms downstairs and a large attic up above. Mr. Carter had come to Ohio a year earlier, soon after the wilderness around Cleveland was first surveyed. He had helped clear the patch of land Seth was crossing and put up the three log cabins. The following year Mr. Carter had brought his family out from Connecticut, and later he persuaded friends like Seth's father and Mr. Stiles to join him in building the new settlement.

Lorenzo Carter operated a store in one of his cabin's downstairs rooms. He sold sugar, salt, and cloth to the other settlers, and traded for furs with the Indian hunters who sometimes passed through Cleveland. Seth wished he could stop now at Carter's store for a piece of hard candy. But there wasn't time if he meant to get to the mill before noon.

Just past the Carter cabin, the little settlement came to an abrupt end. As Seth approached the thick wall of forest that surrounded it on three sides, he couldn't help comparing Cleveland with New Jerusalem, the thriving Connecticut town he and his family had left just a few months ago.

New Jerusalem was built around a grassy common. Two white-frame churches rose at either end of the common, and along its sides stood the town's other main buildings: a tavern, a general store, a blacksmith's shop, and the community's one-room schoolhouse. All day, traffic bustled along the road that circled the common. The wealthy citizens riding in horse-drawn carriages passed farmers driving wagons loaded with produce. Seth couldn't understand why his parents had wanted to move away from such a lively place.

Leaving the sunlit clearing, he started up a narrow path that led through the shadowy forest. The path had been made by the Eries, the Indian tribe that once lived in the region. Most of the Eries had been killed in a bloody war with another tribe, the Iroquois. As he climbed upward, Seth heard a rumbling noise to his right. He wondered if the ghosts of the Eries had returned to haunt the woods, and he walked a little faster.

Halfway to the mill, Seth came to an opening in the trees. It would be a good spot to catch his breath and rest for a moment. He lowered the sack of corn and turned to look back down the path. From this height he could see the three cabins in the clearing. How small they seemed!

Beside the settlement flowed the Cuyahoga River. And beyond the river Lake Erie shimmered in the sun. Because no roads had been cut through the wilderness, Seth and his family had traveled to Cleveland by flatboat along the southern shore of the lake. He remembered how glad they'd all been when Mr. Doan guided the boat into the river and they saw the cabins of Cleveland up ahead.

This morning there were no boats on the lake, no signs of life anywhere. Seth felt a sudden, sharp pang of loneliness. He remembered his brothers who had died. And he thought of all the people he had left behind in Connecticut—his grandparents and friends, especially his best friend, Joseph. Here there were no boys his age to play with. His parents said more families were sure to

come to Cleveland soon. But until they arrived he would have no friends with whom he could go fishing or share a joke.

A songbird's trill roused Seth from his gloomy thoughts. You've got a job to do, he reminded himself. And feeling sad won't help you to do it. He raised the sack of corn to his shoulder and continued on his way.

Seth sighed with relief when he finally saw Judge Kingsbury's mill up ahead. The man had been a judge back in Connecticut, and he kept the title when he moved west even though there were no law courts in Ohio yet. "Hello, Judge!" Seth called out.

The plump little man did not return Seth's greeting. Instead he backed away from him. "You can grind your corn, but don't come close to me," the judge said. "I don't want to catch your sickness!"

"I'm not sick," Seth protested.

"Maybe not, but I hear other people are down with the shakes and fever." The judge backed off even farther. "Oh, I'm glad my wife and I got out

23

of Cleveland in time. That stinking swamp is no fit place to live!"

Seth couldn't help but smile at the judge's way of talking. He knew the Kingsburys had moved the year before to the heights above Cleveland. And the judge never stopped telling anyone who would listen how much healthier it was up there.

Seth carried his sack over to the mill. He had often watched his father grind corn in it, so he knew how to pour just the right amount of corn onto the bottom stone. Then he brought down the upper stone and rocked it back and forth with the handle. Soon he had enough fine meal to fill his sack.

Before he set out for home, Seth rested for a while on a bench. Judge Kingsbury approached him. "You must be hungry," the man said. "And thirsty." He handed Seth a slab of cornbread and a mug of water, then retreated quickly.

"Thank you, Judge," Seth said. After he finished eating, he picked up his sack. It was a long way to Cleveland, and he wanted to get home before the sun started to set.

He was almost there when a crackling sound broke the silence. It came from the trees to his left. Seth stopped, and a shiver of fear ran through him. Had some wild animal made the sound?

Suddenly a giant of a man stepped out onto the path. At the sight of him, Seth relaxed. It was his neighbor Lorenzo Carter. In one hand Mr. Carter carried his musket and in the other a big leather sack.

"Hello there, Seth," Lorenzo Carter said. "Been to the mill, I see."

"Yes," Seth said. "My father's sick with the shakes and fever."

Mr. Carter shook his head. "So many people are," he said sadly. "My little boy's down with it. My wife, too."

The big man reached into his sack and pulled out a fat squirrel. "Hunting was good today," he said. "Here's something for your mother to put in her stewpot."

"She'll be pleased to have it," Seth said. "Thank you, sir."

Lorenzo Carter clapped Seth on the back.

"We'd better stay on our feet, lad," he said. "For if we fall ill, who will see that the others are fed?"

Seth felt a surge of pride as he approached his family's cabin. Lorenzo Carter had treated him like an equal! The giant of Cleveland thought he, Seth Doan, was capable of doing a man's job.

But his pride changed to worry as soon as he entered the cabin. The room was dark and still. Seth's sister and his father were both in their beds. And Seth's mother lay on the big bed beside his father. Her face was as pale as a piece of chalk, and she was breathing heavily.

Even Ma Is Ill

I s that you, Seth?" Mrs. Doan raised herself on the bed.

"Yes, Ma." His voice shook a bit as he asked, "Are you all right?"

"Just a little tired." She forced a smile. "You know me—I never get sick."

Seth hoped she was telling the truth. "I've got the cornmeal," he said. "And Lorenzo Carter gave me a squirrel." Seth held it out for his mother to see.

Mrs. Doan managed to stand. "I'll cook it for

come to Cleveland soon. But until they arrived he would have no friends with whom he could go fishing or share a joke.

A songbird's trill roused Seth from his gloomy thoughts. You've got a job to do, he reminded himself. And feeling sad won't help you to do it. He raised the sack of corn to his shoulder and continued on his way.

Seth sighed with relief when he finally saw Judge Kingsbury's mill up ahead. The man had been a judge back in Connecticut, and he kept the title when he moved west even though there were no law courts in Ohio yet. "Hello, Judge!" Seth called out.

The plump little man did not return Seth's greeting. Instead he backed away from him. "You can grind your corn, but don't come close to me," the judge said. "I don't want to catch your sickness!"

"I'm not sick," Seth protested.

"Maybe not, but I hear other people are down with the shakes and fever." The judge backed off even farther. "Oh, I'm glad my wife and I got out

23

of Cleveland in time. That stinking swamp is no fit place to live!"

Seth couldn't help but smile at the judge's way of talking. He knew the Kingsburys had moved the year before to the heights above Cleveland. And the judge never stopped telling anyone who would listen how much healthier it was up there.

Seth carried his sack over to the mill. He had often watched his father grind corn in it, so he knew how to pour just the right amount of corn onto the bottom stone. Then he brought down the upper stone and rocked it back and forth with the handle. Soon he had enough fine meal to fill his sack.

Before he set out for home, Seth rested for a while on a bench. Judge Kingsbury approached him. "You must be hungry," the man said. "And thirsty." He handed Seth a slab of cornbread and a mug of water, then retreated quickly.

"Thank you, Judge," Seth said. After he finished eating, he picked up his sack. It was a long way to Cleveland, and he wanted to get home before the sun started to set.

He was almost there when a crackling sound broke the silence. It came from the trees to his left. Seth stopped, and a shiver of fear ran through him. Had some wild animal made the sound?

Suddenly a giant of a man stepped out onto the path. At the sight of him, Seth relaxed. It was his neighbor Lorenzo Carter. In one hand Mr. Carter carried his musket and in the other a big leather sack.

"Hello there, Seth," Lorenzo Carter said. "Been to the mill, I see."

"Yes," Seth said. "My father's sick with the shakes and fever."

Mr. Carter shook his head. "So many people are," he said sadly. "My little boy's down with it. My wife, too."

The big man reached into his sack and pulled out a fat squirrel. "Hunting was good today," he said. "Here's something for your mother to put in her stewpot."

"She'll be pleased to have it," Seth said. "Thank you, sir."

Lorenzo Carter clapped Seth on the back.

"We'd better stay on our feet, lad," he said. "For if we fall ill, who will see that the others are fed?"

Seth felt a surge of pride as he approached his family's cabin. Lorenzo Carter had treated him like an equal! The giant of Cleveland thought he, Seth Doan, was capable of doing a man's job.

But his pride changed to worry as soon as he entered the cabin. The room was dark and still. Seth's sister and his father were both in their beds. And Seth's mother lay on the big bed beside his father. Her face was as pale as a piece of chalk, and she was breathing heavily.

Even Ma Is Ill

Is that you, Seth?" Mrs. Doan raised herself on the bed.

"Yes, Ma." His voice shook a bit as he asked, "Are you all right?"

"Just a little tired." She forced a smile. "You know me—I never get sick."

Seth hoped she was telling the truth. "I've got the cornmeal," he said. "And Lorenzo Carter gave me a squirrel." Seth held it out for his mother to see.

Mrs. Doan managed to stand. "I'll cook it for

supper." She started across the room toward the fireplace. Looking at her, Seth was afraid she wouldn't have the strength to cook the squirrel. "I'll skin it for you, Ma," he said.

Seth did more than that. After he skinned the animal, he cut it into pieces. Then he got the fire going and helped his mother to cook it. He pretended not to notice when she had to lean against the chimney stones for support.

While the squirrel was sizzling, his mother showed Seth how to mix the cornmeal with milk to make cornbread. Then he helped serve the food to his father and sister.

Mercy ate some of the meat and bread, but Mr. Doan took only a few bites. He thought he was back in their old home in Connecticut. "On Saturday we'll go to the fair in New Haven," he told Seth.

Mrs. Doan didn't eat much either. And she lay down on the bed again as soon as she had finished.

Seth covered the fire with ashes and climbed

the ladder to the attic. His mind raced as he tried to fall asleep. And when sleep finally came, it brought a bad dream with it.

In the dream, Seth was walking through a wood with his family when it started to snow. It snowed and snowed, but he and the others didn't stop. They ducked their heads to escape the icy wind, and plodded on.

After some time, the wind died down. Seth raised his head to look around. Where were the others? He swung his gaze in every direction, but they had all vanished—his sister, his mother, and his father. He was all alone in the darkening wood. And the snow kept on drifting down. . . .

Seth woke in a cold sweat. He smiled when he realized it was only a dream. But it was a long time before he fell asleep again.

The next morning, his mother was too weak to get out of bed. When she tried, her entire body began to shiver and shake. Seth watched help-lessly as the attack continued. After about twenty minutes, the shivering stopped. But then a high fever swept his mother's body.

Seth bathed her forehead with cool water. There was no doubt about it now—Ma had the shakes and fever, too. Like it or not, he was the only one left to look after his family.

First, Seth milked the cow they had brought with them all the way from Connecticut. She had been tied behind their wagon as far as Buffalo and then tethered to a stake on the flatboat. The Doans had had to leave their horse and wagon with friends in Buffalo because there were no roads beyond that point.

With the fresh milk, Seth made cornmeal mush and got his father and sister to eat a little. His mother had no appetite. After the others had finished, Seth ate a heaping bowl himself. He would need all his strength if he was to see his family through this terrible sickness. And he'd never be able to do it if he didn't stay well himself.

He was getting ready to go to the mill for more cornmeal when there was a knock on the door. It was Mrs. Stiles from the cabin next door.

She seemed surprised to see Seth, and he was

afraid she was going to say something about the damage he'd done to her petunias. Instead, she looked to either side of him and asked, "Where's your mother?"

"She's taken sick," Seth said.

"Who hasn't?" Mrs. Stiles sighed. "We're out of meal, and my Jeb's too weak to go to the mill." She held out a sack of corn. "I was wondering if you could grind some for us?"

She looked so pitiful Seth had to say yes.

"Thank you, Seth. It will be my family's salvation!"

After Mrs. Stiles left, Seth grabbed hold of the two sacks of corn and set out for the mill. The weight of his load made the trip seem twice as long. Seth shifted the sacks from one arm to the other and stopped to rest three times along the way. He was gasping for breath when he finally reached the mill.

On the way home, he hoped he'd run into Lorenzo Carter again. But there was no sign of the big, cheerful man.

The next morning Seth found out why. When Mrs. Stiles came to the cabin, she told him Lorenzo Carter had fallen ill, too.

She held out two sacks of corn. "We'd be much obliged, Seth, if you could grind this corn for us." Her eyes had a pleading look. "One sack is for me, and the other is for the Carters."

Seth nodded, but said nothing.

After Mrs. Stiles had gone, he let out a sigh that was more like a groan. He didn't know if he could carry three full sacks by himself. It would have been easy if his family still had their horse and wagon. Then he could have driven to the mill. But they didn't—and besides, there was no road.

What was it Lorenzo Carter had said? "We'd better stay on our feet, lad. For if we fall ill, who will see that the others are fed?" Well, Mr. Carter was sick now, and he, Seth, was the only one left to get food for the settlement. Without something to eat, his family and his neighbors would not be able to throw off the shakes and fever.

They'd just get weaker and weaker. And some of them might die.

The bad dream flashed again before Seth's eyes. He could see himself alone in his cabin, the last person left alive in Cleveland. Hungry wolves howled as they crept out of the woods and headed toward his front door. They started to scrape against it with their claws and . . .

Seth shook his head fiercely. You mustn't think such things, he told himself. The mill—that's all you can afford to think about. Getting to the mill and back again with the food everyone needs. He took a deep breath, slowly lifted the three heavy sacks of corn, and stumbled up the path.

CHAPTER SIX

The Bear

It was hard to keep the three sacks in balance. Seth started out carrying two sacks in his left hand and one in his right. But before he'd gone even a mile he had to stop and shift them around. For the next half mile or so, he carried two in his right hand and one in his left. Then he shifted them around again before climbing the final slope to the mill.

Judge Kingsbury was nowhere in sight. That didn't surprise Seth; the worried little man had been avoiding him ever since the first morning. But the judge never failed to leave a slab of cornbread and a cup of water for Seth on the bench.

Seth thought the trip downhill with the three sacks of cornmeal would be easier, but he was wrong. His shoulders and wrists still ached from the trip to the mill, and he had to stop more often to rest. He had just put the sacks down for the third time and was rubbing his tired shoulders when he heard a noise. Something was tramping through the woods up ahead to his right. He listened hard; yes, it was coming closer.

Seth froze. Before when he'd heard sounds like that it had turned out to be Lorenzo Carter. But today Mr. Carter was in bed with the shakes and fever. If he hadn't had the sacks to carry, Seth might have turned and run back up the path. Now he could do nothing but wait to see what was making so much noise.

It wasn't long before he found out. A middle-size black bear—probably a yearling—lumbered out of the woods in front of Seth. It looked toward him and let out a low growl.

Seth's jaw tightened and his legs quivered, but he stayed where he was. He remembered a piece of advice his father had given him: "If a wild animal surprises you, Seth, don't make a move. That may alarm the creature. Just stand your ground and pray that it goes away."

The bear took a step toward Seth, growled again, and sniffed the air. Did it smell the cornmeal in the sacks? Seth wondered. Was it hungry? Now Seth's arms were quivering, too, but still he didn't move.

For a long moment the bear held Seth in its gaze. Then, as if deciding he was no threat, the animal abruptly swung away from him. It shuffled back into the woods, snapping twigs as it went.

Once the bear had gone, Seth dropped to his knees in the middle of the path and let out the breath he'd been holding. He stayed there on the ground until his limbs stopped shaking, then rose slowly to his feet. Taking up the three sacks again, he continued on his way. For some reason, his load didn't seem as heavy as it had before.

Seth didn't say anything about his encounter with the bear when he got home. He figured it would only upset his parents and Mercy—if they

even understood what he was talking about. They were still so sick.

For the next week, Seth took three sacks of corn to the mill every morning and brought back three sacks of meal every afternoon. Between trips, he looked after his family as best he could. He made mush and cornbread for them to eat, and carried water from the spring for them to drink. He bathed their feverish bodies and emptied their smelly slopjars. Whenever they felt like it, he talked with them. And sometimes they told him things he hadn't known before.

One morning, when her shaking spells let up for a while, his mother turned to him and said, "I'm sorry if I seemed to criticize you for wanting to read, Seth." She took his hand. "Remember how I taught you to read, and how we used to enjoy reading together?"

Seth nodded.

"You don't know how much I miss having time to read myself," his mother said. "And when I think of all the books we had to leave behind . . ." Her voice cracked and tears moistened her eyes.

"Don't cry, Ma," Seth said. "I understand."

Another time it was his sister's turn. "Will I ever feel well again?" Mercy moaned one afternoon while Seth was bathing her face. "I don't know why I *want* to get well, though. I hate this place! There's no one to talk to—no boys to dance with!"

Seth tried to console her. "Don't worry, Mercy. More families are sure to come soon. Papa said so. And you'll want to be well when they get here, won't you?"

"Oh, what do you know?" Mercy snapped. "It could be months before anyone else comes to Cleveland—years! And by then I'll be a dried-up old maid!"

Seth had no answer to that. Mercy was exaggerating—she always did. But he knew what she meant about Cleveland. It was a lonely place for everyone.

The hardest conversation, though, was one he had with his father. Mr. Doan had insisted on getting out of bed, and Seth was trying to get him to eat a little mush. His father kept brushing the spoon aside. He had something urgent on his mind, and he was determined to get it out.

"I want to talk to you seriously," he said, keeping his voice low so only Seth could hear what he said. "If I should die, here's what you must do—"

"Pa, don't even say it!" Seth interrupted.

"Hush, and listen to me, son. You must take your mother and Mercy and go back to Connecticut. Our friends in Buffalo will help you—"

"Pa, please. You're going to get well. I know you are!"

His father ignored him. Beads of sweat stood out on his forehead as he continued. "I probably should never have brought you all out here. But I didn't have much choice. When your grandpa dies, your Uncle Benjamin will inherit the family farm. I couldn't see working for my brother, so I decided to take my chances out here. And look what it got me. . . ."

"It'll work out, Pa," Seth said, wishing with all his strength that it were true. "You'll see."

"But if it doesn't, I want you to promise me that you'll go back to Connecticut. Your grandpa and your uncle will see that all of you are looked after, and you'll grow up to be a fine young man."

"Pa, please—"

"Promise me, Seth!" His father's eyes had a pleading look.

"I promise," Seth whispered. What else could he say? He tried to keep his hand steady as he dipped the spoon into the bowl of mush and extended it once more toward his father. "Now please try to eat a little something."

CHAPTER SEVEN

The Sacks Are So Heavy

Seth's father ate a few bites, then stumbled back to bed and quickly fell asleep. After checking briefly on his mother and sister, Seth climbed the ladder to his mattress in the attic. He blew out the candle and stretched out on the straw mattress. How good it felt to lie down!

But even though every muscle in his body cried for rest, his mind refused to stop working. His father's words kept echoing in his thoughts: "If I should die, here's what you must do . . . must do . . . must do . . ." Was there really a danger that his father would die? And what about his mother? And Mercy? Up till now it was only in his dreams that Seth had felt threatened. But tonight the possibility that he would be left alone here in the wilderness seemed all too real. The mere idea of it made him shudder.

At last he gave up trying to sleep and relit his candle. Fearful of fire, he set the candle at a safe distance from the mattress. Then he reached for the Bible, which he'd brought up from downstairs. At times like these, reading was the only way he could forget his doubts and fears, at least for the moment. He prayed it would work its spell again tonight.

He looked for a passage where the Lord helped people in trouble. One of his favorites was from the book of Isaiah. Yes, here it was! "Even the youths shall faint and be weary, and the young men shall utterly fall: But they that wait upon the Lord shall renew their strength; they shall mount up with wings as eagles; they shall run, and not be weary; and they shall walk, and not faint."

As Seth read the familiar words, he felt the Bible was speaking directly to him. The words had always reassured him, but tonight they had a stronger effect than ever. His body relaxed, and his eyelids started to droop. He put down the book, blew out the candle, and lay back on the mattress. A smile was on his lips as he drifted into sleep.

When he woke up the next morning, no sounds greeted him from downstairs. He jumped up from the mattress, pulled on his pants, and hurried over to the ladder. Had his parents and sister gotten worse overnight? No, he found them all breathing peacefully when he climbed down into the cabin.

His neighbors seemed better, too, when he stopped by to get their sacks of corn. Mrs. Stiles was up and dressed and baking a fresh supply of cornbread. "I don't think you'll have to do for us much longer, Seth," she said. And then she surprised him by apologizing for being so hard on him about her flowers.

"I'm ashamed of the way I yelled at you that

day," she said. "But I brought those petunia plants all the way from Buffalo. They're all I have to remind me of the beautiful garden I had back home."

"I know, Mrs. Stiles," Seth said. "And I'm sorry I stomped on them."

"Never mind, Seth." She patted his arm. "You've more than made up for it, believe me."

Her words filled Seth with a happy glow as he walked on to Lorenzo Carter's place. But they also made him realize what Mrs. Stiles had lost when she came to Cleveland. Up till then he'd been aware only of his own loneliness in the remote settlement. But now, after listening to his mother and father and sister—and Mrs. Stiles—he could could see how much everyone had given up when they moved west.

Lorenzo Carter was in the midst of a loud argument with his wife when Seth approached their cabin. "I'm telling you I'm better," Mr. Carter shouted to Mrs. Carter as he struggled into his clothes. "And I won't have that poor young fellow lugging my corn to the mill!" Just then Seth came through the door.

"Oh, hello, Seth," Mr. Carter said. "As you can tell, we were just talking about you, and I was saying—" At that point, the man's face suddenly reddened and he was overcome by one racking cough after another.

"You see what I mean?" Mrs. Carter said. "You're better, yes, but you're certainly not well enough to go to the mill."

Seth looked on as she led her husband back to the big four-poster bed that occupied one end of the room. "Now just get out of those clothes and give yourself another day of rest."

"I tell you I can make it!" Mr. Carter started to say, but another spell of coughing cut him short. "I'm sorry, son," he said to Seth when he got his breath again. "But I guess my missus is right—I'd better give myself another day of rest."

"That's all right, sir," Seth said. "I've gotten used to the trip by now." He added the Carters' sack of corn to the other two he was carrying, took a long, deep breath, and started up the path to the mill.

When he came home that afternoon, he was surprised to find Mercy outside the cabin, milking their cow. "I decided that it was time I started making myself useful again," she said, looking more like her old self than she had in weeks.

Seth couldn't have been more pleased. The trip to the mill that day had been especially tiring for some reason, and he welcomed a chance to lie down for a while before supper. He was so tired that he didn't even think of reading a passage or two in the Bible before stretching out on his mattress.

The next morning he felt cold when he got up even though it was another hot August day. Then a sudden fit of chills shook his body as he was getting dressed. He wished he could lie back down and sleep for another hour, but he knew that wasn't possible. Mercy and Mrs. Stiles might be getting better, but everyone else was still sick. And they still needed him to bring them their daily supply of food.

He didn't say anything about the chills when he went downstairs. However, Mercy noticed that he wasn't eating his breakfast mush. "Are you all right?" she asked.

"I'm fine," he lied. "Just tired of mush is all."

He filled their sack with corn, then stopped at the Stiles and Carter cabins for the other two sacks. Sweat poured from him as he climbed the path to the mill. "Am I getting the shakes and fever, too?" he asked himself. He shoved that frightening thought aside and kept on climbing.

At the mill, Seth ground all the corn and measured it carefully into the three sacks. It was hard because his hands were shaking. He sipped some of the water Judge Kingsbury had left for him, but he didn't have any appetite for the corn-bread. Then, hoisting the sacks, he started down the path toward home.

The sacks felt heavier than ever. He kept putting them down and picking them up. His thoughts were confused, and his body felt as if it were on fire. At last he stopped to rest on the trunk of a fallen tree. When he finally got up again, his head started to whirl. The trees seemed to be doing a dance around him.

Off in the woods somewhere, an animal growled. Was it a wolf, or maybe another bear? Seth looked around nervously. Where was his mother? His father? His sister? Hadn't they started down the path with him? Or had that happened in a dream? Seth didn't know anymore what was real and what was not.

Ahead he could see the cabins of Cleveland through the trees. He forced his legs to move faster. That was when the seizure struck him. Suddenly every part of his body began to shake violently. He tightened his grip on the sacks of meal, but it was no use. He felt himself falling . . . falling. . . .

The black bear was chasing him through the woods. Seth ducked behind a tree and struggled to catch his breath. Had he managed to escape from the creature? He peered around the tree and was overcome with fright. There was the bear, only a few feet away. The animal saw him and let out a fierce growl. Then it lunged.

Seth woke with a start and looked around dazedly. He was in the cabin, lying on Mercy's pallet, and his father was bending over him. "What happened?" Seth asked.

"You fainted on the path."

"How did I get home?"

"I managed to carry you." His father smoothed out Seth's blanket. "When you didn't come back, I was worried and went in search. Luckily I found you right away."

"The cornmeal . . . what happened to it?"

"Mercy brought back the three sacks. Only a little spilled."

Tears came to Seth's eyes. "I was so close to home, but I didn't get here. I let you all down . . . I failed!"

"You didn't fail," his father said. "That's just the fever talking."

Mr. Doan bent down to kiss his son on the

forehead. "Your mother was right. You're a lot stronger than I ever gave you credit for."

Had he heard right? Seth wondered. Did his father really think he was strong? He had no chance to ask any more questions, though. A fresh wave of chills swept across his body, and his teeth chattered so much that he couldn't speak.

CHAPTER EIGHT

A Wonderful Present

Three weeks passed before the chills stopped and Seth began to feel like himself again. By then all the other settlers had recovered from the shakes and fever, too.

"We should do something to celebrate our good fortune," said Lorenzo Carter. And so, on a sunny Saturday in September, everyone in Cleveland trooped down to the shore of Lake Erie for a picnic.

Shrieks and giggles filled the air as the Carters' little boy and the two Stiles girls played hide-and-seek amid the rocks on the beach. Seth was too old for hide-and-seek. Instead he helped his mother and sister carry bowls of food to the picnic site. Then he walked over to where his father and the other men were talking with two strangers.

The strangers had arrived unexpectedly in Cleveland the day before. First, the settlers had heard the sound of axes slashing through the underbrush. Then, two men had appeared at the edge of the clearing, leading a supply wagon drawn by a pair of oxen. They told the startled settlers they had hacked a road through the forest all the way from Conneaut, seventy miles to the east.

"We started out in early May," the older of the two men was saying now.

"We stayed close to the lake," his younger partner added. "And we followed old Iroquois trails wherever we could."

"But sometimes they faded out, and we had to chop our way through the trees," the older man concluded.

"The important thing is that you got through,"

Lorenzo Carter said. "Now settlers will have two ways to get to Cleveland—by water along the lake shore and by land, thanks to your new road."

"And more people are sure to come," Mr. Stiles said. "Where else can they find good land as cheap as it is out here?"

"Maybe we'll get a doctor," Seth's father added hopefully. "And a schoolmaster for our children."

"And a preacher," Lorenzo Carter said. "Every town needs a good preacher."

And maybe there'll be some boys my age to play with, Seth thought. Boys who will be my friends.

"Time to eat!" called Mrs. Stiles.

She and the other women had spread out the bowls and plates of food on a flat stretch of ground just above the beach. There were venison haunches from the deer that Seth's father and Mr. Carter had hunted. Mr. Stiles had contributed fish from the lake. Mrs. Stiles had baked cornbread, and Seth's mother had made her own special corn pudding. To top off the feast, Mrs. Carter had baked a plum cake with flour from her husband's store.

Seth glanced from one person to another as he ate his dessert. How different they looked from a month ago! Then, his sister had wailed about being an old maid; now, Mercy was chatting happily with one of the men who'd come from the East. Then, his father had been afraid he was dying; now, he and the other grown-ups were excited about the future of Cleveland. As for Seth, he'd wondered if he'd ever throw off the shakes and fever that had him in its grip. Now, he had a hard time remembering what it was like to be sick.

After the last bit of cake had disappeared, Lorenzo Carter stood up. He lifted his glass of wild blackberry juice and proposed a toast. "To Seth Doan," he said, "a lad brave and true. If it weren't for him, and the food he brought us, it's not likely we'd be here today, enjoying this fine picnic."

Everyone cheered, and Seth blushed. Praise like Mr. Carter's was nice to hear, but it made Seth feel shy.

Mr. Carter had more to say, though. "To show our appreciation for what you did, Seth, we'd like to give you this present." He reached down to the ground and picked up a package wrapped in brown paper.

As everyone clapped, Seth ducked his head. He didn't know what he was supposed to do.

"Come on up here, lad," Mr. Carter said with a smile. "Otherwise we may think you don't want your present."

"Go on, son," his mother urged.

At last Seth stood up and walked over to Lorenzo Carter. The big man clasped his shoulder and handed him the package. "We all know what a good reader you are," he said. "So we hope you'll enjoy what's inside."

"Thank you, Mr. Carter," Seth said. He stared at the package and ran his fingers over the edges. Could it be what Mr. Carter had hinted at? No, that wasn't possible. . . .

"Well, aren't you going to open it?" Mr. Carter said.

Seth carefully unwrapped the brown paper, and there it was—the present he hadn't thought possible. A book. A fine, thick book bound in red

leather with the title printed in gold on the cover: *The Life and Strange, Surprising Adventures of Robinson Crusoe, of York, Mariner.*

Seth couldn't believe it. A book of his very own. And something new to read. What could be more wonderful? He clasped the book to his chest. "Thank you," he said again. "Thank you all!"

Mr. Stiles took out his harmonica and began to play a jolly tune. Everyone crowded around Seth, wanting to get a glimpse of his book. His mother admired the handsome binding. One of the young men who'd blazed the road from Conneaut said, "That book came all the way from the East. We brought it with us in our wagon."

But Seth wasn't interested just then in where the book had come from. All he wanted was to go off somewhere by himself, open his marvelous gift, and start to read about Robinson Crusoe and his strange, surprising adventures.

AUTHOR'S NOTE

This story is a work of fiction, but Seth Doan was a real boy, and Lorenzo Carter, the Stileses, and Judge Kingsbury were real people, too. They were among the first settlers of Cleveland, Ohio. Seth and his family arrived in the little frontier community in the spring of 1798, a few months before the start of the story.

When Seth and the others came to Cleveland, the northeastern part of Ohio was known as the Western Reserve of Connecticut. Ohio didn't become a state until 1803. The Reserve had been surveyed in 1796 by Moses Cleaveland, who also established the first permanent settlement in the region. From then on Cleveland bore his name—minus one *a*—even though he didn't live there.

The shakes and fever—also known as the ague—was a form of malaria. It struck Cleveland in the late summer of

1798, probably spread by mosquitoes. The real Seth Doan, like the boy in the story, kept everyone in Cleveland fed during the epidemic. Thanks to his efforts, no one in the settlement died.

Shortly after the epidemic ended, a road from the East was cut through to Cleveland, as described in the story. After that, the little settlement was linked more directly to the outside world. Never again would its existence be threatened as it was in that summer of 1798.

When the real Seth Doan grew up, he served for many years as county sheriff. He lived to see Cleveland grow from a cluster of cabins to one of the major cities in the United States.